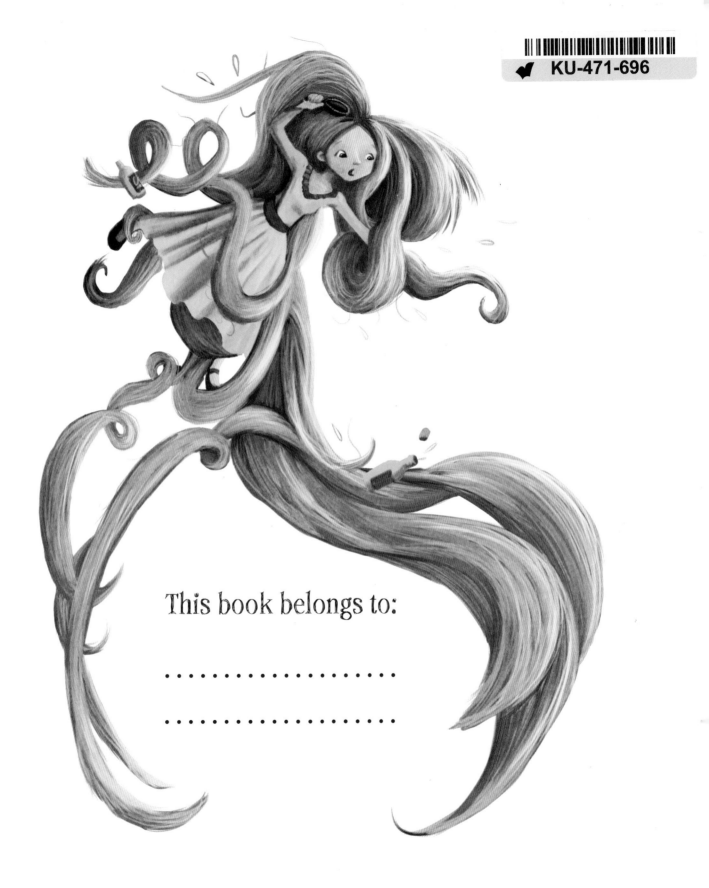

This book belongs to:

. . . .

. . . .

Editor: Carly Madden

Designer: Hannah Mason

Series Designer: Victoria Kimonidou

Editorial Director: Victoria Garrard

Art Director: Laura Roberts-Jensen

Copyright © QED Publishing 2016

A NEW BURLINGTON BOOK

First published in hardback in the UK in 2015

by QED Publishing

Part of The Quarto Group

The Old Brewery, 6 Blundell Street, London N7 9BH

MIX
Paper from
responsible sources
FSC® C016973
FSC
www.fsc.org

A catalogue record for this book is available from the British Library.

ISBN 978 1 78493 802 4

Printed in China

Rapunzel, Rapunzel, WASH YOUR HAIR!

Written by Steve Smallman

Illustrated by Neil Price

NEW BURLINGTON

Once upon a time there was a young
girl called Rapunzel who had
really,

really

long

hair!

She'd been kidnapped by a wicked witch who kept her in a room at the top of a very tall tower.

The tower had no staircase and no front door!

The wicked witch used
Rapunzel's hair as a rope to
climb up and down the tower.

When she needed to
climb up she cried,
"Rapunzel, Rapunzel,
let down your
golden hair!"

The hair fell down and
the witch climbed up.
OUCH!

Poor Rapunzel never went out at all.
She was sad, lonely...

...and very hairy!

Having so much hair was hard work.

Rapunzel was always tripping over her hair.

It was such an effort to wash and brush that, after a while, she just didn't bother!

She sat by the
window daydreaming
about being rescued
by a handsome prince.
Her hair got dirtier
and dirtier.

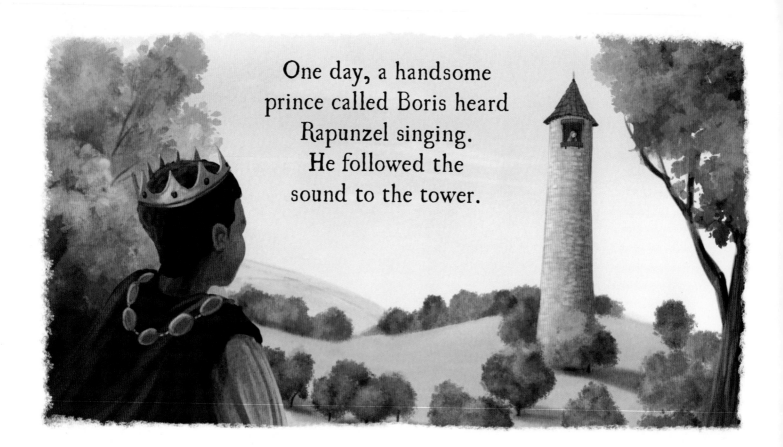

One day, a handsome
prince called Boris heard
Rapunzel singing.
He followed the
sound to the tower.

He tried to climb
the tower but it was
too smooth and he
couldn't get a grip!

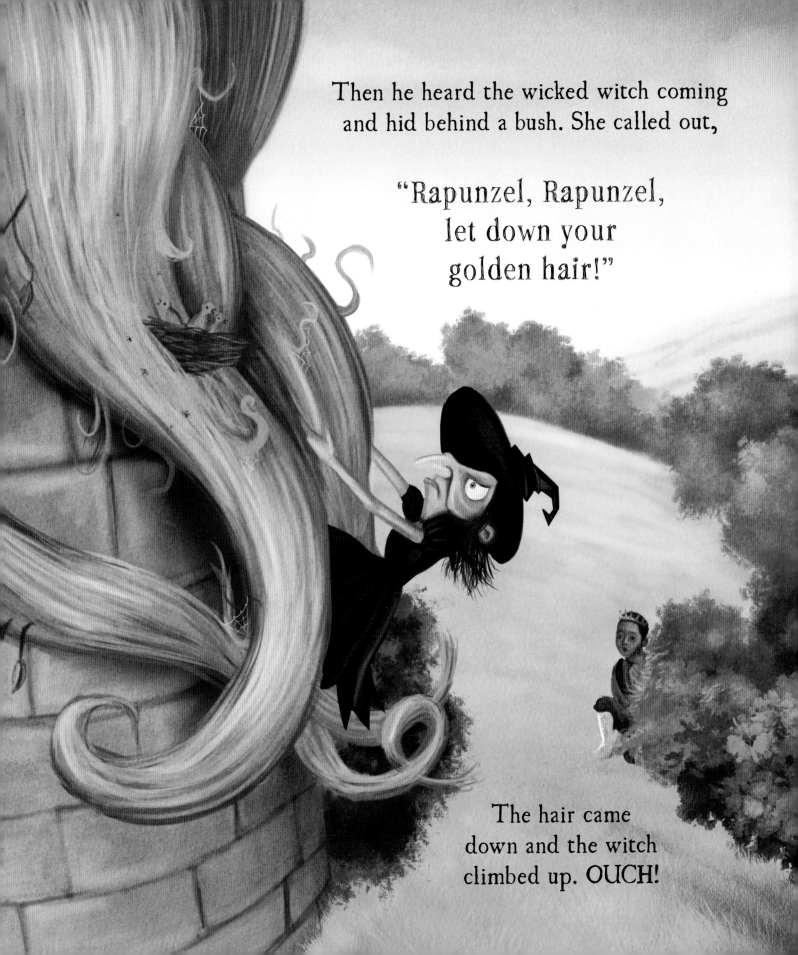

Then he heard the wicked witch coming and hid behind a bush. She called out,

"Rapunzel, Rapunzel, let down your golden hair!"

The hair came down and the witch climbed up. OUCH!

Boris waited for the witch to climb back down.
Then, when he was sure she was gone,
he sneaked up to the tower and in his best
'wicked witch' voice cried,

"Rapunzel, Rapunzel,
let down your
golden hair!"

The hair came down
but it was filthy.

"Yuck!" he cried.
"I'm not climbing
up that!"

He stomped off
in a huff!

A few days later, another prince came along.

Albert had heard about the girl in
the tower with the lovely voice
and the disgusting hair.

So he came to rescue her...
with gloves on. He called out,
"Rapunzel, Rapunzel,
let down your
golden hair!"

The hair came down and
he started climbing up...

...but halfway up
the tower, his head
started to itch!
He'd caught
head lice from
Rapunzel's hair!

He let go of her hair to
scratch his head and fell
back down with a thump!
He gave up and left.

Rapunzel's hair got so grubby
and grim that even the
witch couldn't stand
it anymore.

"I'm leaving!"
screeched the witch.
"And I won't
be coming back!"

She climbed down Rapunzel's
hair for the last time.

It was so greasy
that she lost her grip
and slipped to the bottom
of the tower with a
SPLAT!

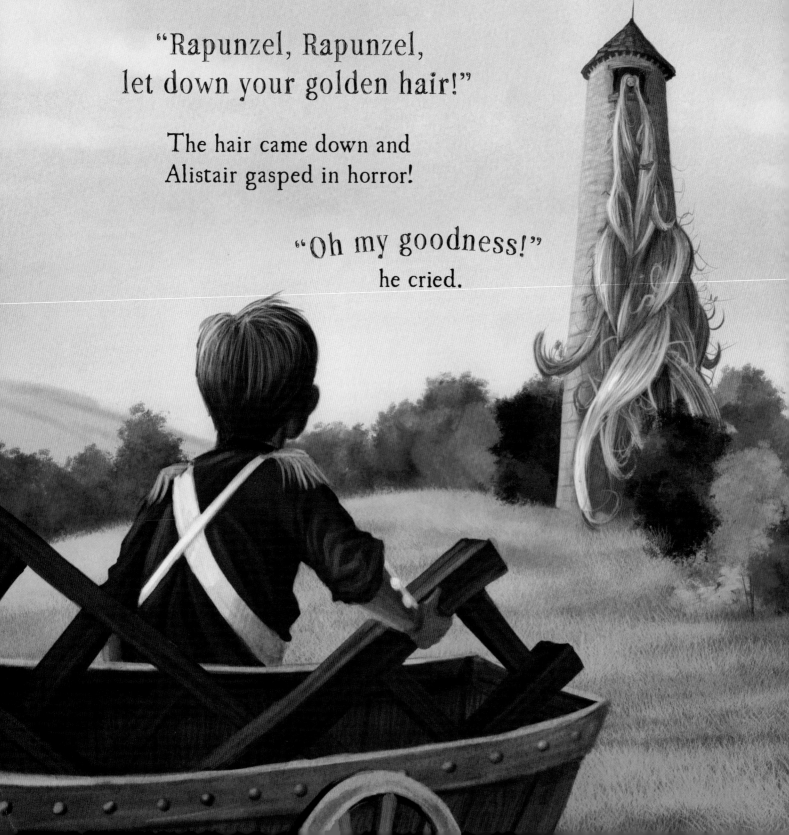

Soon another prince came along. His name was
Alistair and he had a ladder. He called out,

"Rapunzel, Rapunzel,
let down your golden hair!"

The hair came down and
Alistair gasped in horror!

"Oh my goodness!"
he cried.

"Your hair needs rescuing more than you do! When did you last use shampoo?"

He fetched a hosepipe, head-lice lotion, shampoo, conditioner...

...and a selection of brushes and combs.

Alistair set to work!

It took all day, but by the time Alistair had finished,
Rapunzel's hair was clean, shiny, golden and beautiful.

Then the prince
helped Rapunzel
climb out of
the tower.

"Oh, thank you, my
handsome prince!"
sighed Rapunzel.

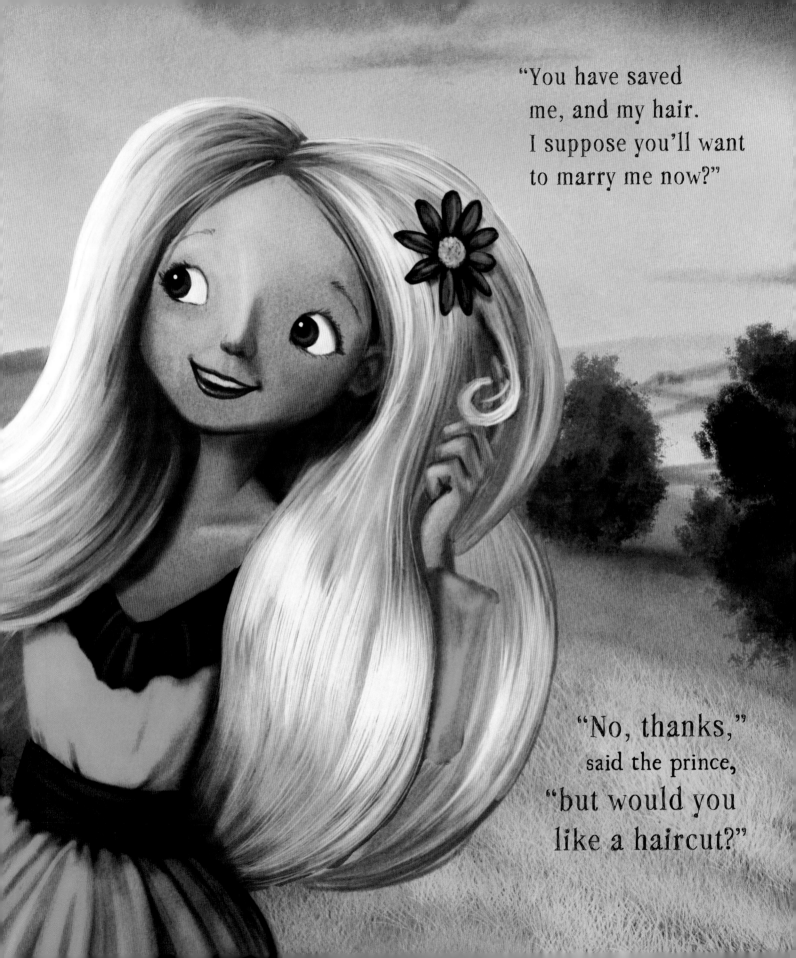

"You have saved me, and my hair. I suppose you'll want to marry me now?"

"No, thanks," said the prince, "but would you like a haircut?"

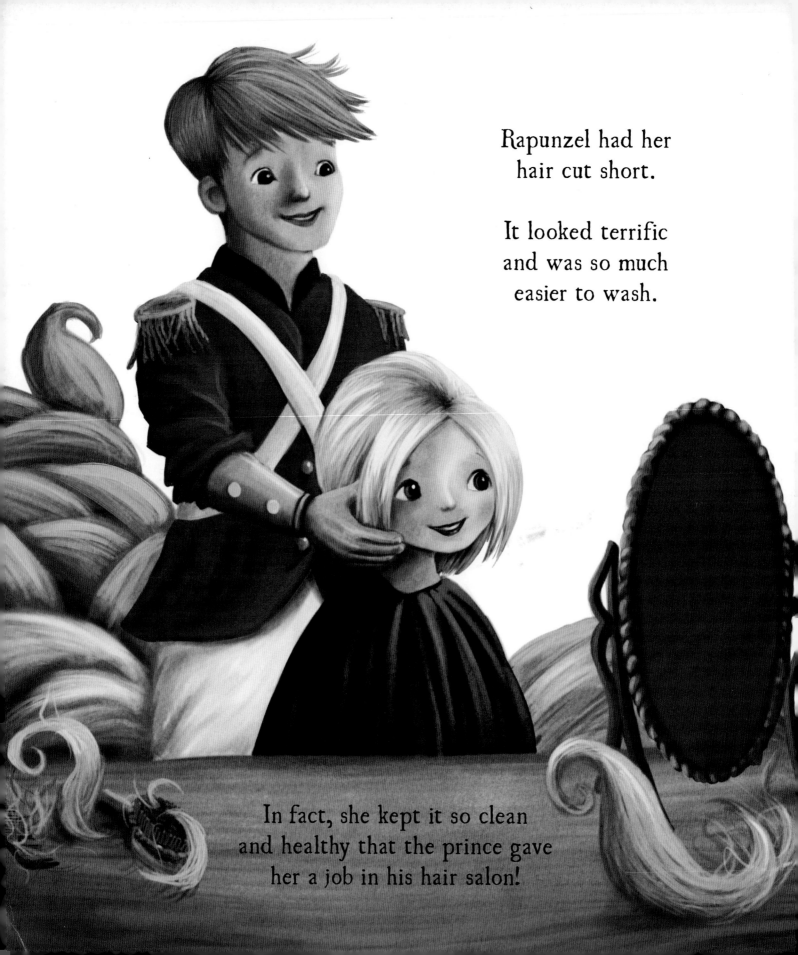

Rapunzel had her
hair cut short.

It looked terrific
and was so much
easier to wash.

In fact, she kept it so clean
and healthy that the prince gave
her a job in his hair salon!

Prince Alistair used Rapunzel's leftover hair
to make wigs and moustaches for all the
bald people of the kingdom...

With Your Hair!

Wigs
For
Sale!

...who all lived happily
and hairily ever after!

Next steps

Show the children the cover again. When they first saw it, did they think that they already knew the story? How is this story different from the traditional story? Which bits are the same?

Rapunzel's hair was really long. Ask the children to imagine what it would be like to have hair that length. Would it be easy to look after? How long would it take to wash and brush? What if it got tangles in it?

In this story, did Rapunzel look after her hair? Ask the children what they think it would feel like to have really dirty hair.

What happened when the first prince saw Rapunzel's hair? What did he say?

What happened when the second prince tried to climb up Rapunzel's hair?

When the third prince came along, what did the children think he would do when he saw Rapunzel's yucky hair? What did he actually do?

When Prince Alistair had washed and brushed Rapunzel's hair, how did it look? How did Rapunzel feel?

Ask the children to draw a picture of themselves with really long hair like Rapunzel. Or they could draw themselves with a really big moustache – like the ones that Alistair made with Rapunzel's leftover hair!